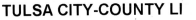

That EGG is MINE!

Liz Goulet Dubois

sourcebooks jabberwocky

4

7

It bumped.

It flew!

and
rolled...

and rolled...

and **PLUNKED** into the pond!

I am a good swimmer,
so I got it back.

For Mom and Dad, who've watched my
humble childhood chicken scratches turn into books.
Thanks for the art supplies, and everything else.

—LGD.

Prismacolor pencils and Adobe Photoshop were used to prepare the full color art.

Published by Sourcebooks Jabberwocky, an imprint of Sourcebooks Kids
P.O. Box 4410, Naperville, Illinois 60567–4410
(630) 961-3900
sourcebookskids.com

Library of Congress Cataloging-in-Publication Data is on file with the publisher.

Source of Production: Phoenix Color, Hagerstown, Maryland, USA
Date of Production: August 2021
Run Number: 5022979

Printed and bound in the United States of America.
PHC 10 9 8 7 6 5 4 3 2 1